Why Hummingbird

A Hitchiti Indian Pourquoi

retold by Cynthia Swain
illustrated by Lisa and Terry Workman

Long ago, Heron and Hummingbird hunted
in the same lakes and rivers for fish.
The birds became friends, but they
were as different as night and day.

Heron was big and slow, and his wings
were wide. His talent was that he could
fly a long time without stopping. Heron
had a huge appetite. He ate loads of
fish every day to nourish his body.

3

Hummingbird was tinier than a mouse, and she had small but speedy wings. Her talent was that she could fly fast. She could also fly backward! Hummingbird also ate fish, but only a couple each day. Hummingbird feared that Heron might devour all of the fish!

So Hummingbird came up with a plan and challenged Heron to a race. "Whoever wins will own the waters and can have all of the fish. Do you accept?" she inquired.

Heron sighed. He disliked betting, but he agreed.

The birds would fly over a forest and a lake. Whoever got to the far side of the lake first would win the right to own the rivers and lakes. Hummingbird took off first. She soared into the sky. Her wings flapped so quickly a humming sound could be heard throughout the forest.

Heron was still on the ground.
Then he began to slowly flap his large
wings. Finally, he took off into the sky.

After a while, Hummingbird was miles ahead, zigzagging about. She grew hungry. Flapping her wings was hard work! A sea of red trumpet flowers swam below her.

Hummingbird flew down. She tasted the nectar of each flower. "YUM!" she cried, her tongue dancing with joy. Hummingbird drank nectar for hours. When she looked up, she saw that Heron was now ahead of her.

"YIKES!" called the tiny bird. She flapped her wings faster and faster and finally passed Heron. When night fell, Hummingbird was exhausted. She found a tree to nestle in, and she slept soundly.

Heron flew through the night. He flew slowly. He flew steadily.

When Hummingbird awoke, she was hungry again. She found a garden of red roses. She sipped nectar all morning.

When she looked into the sky, Heron was nowhere around. "Heron must have given up," Hummingbird said happily.

"I am about to win. I will drink some more nectar."

Hummingbird did not get to the far side of the lake until the afternoon. Heron was sitting in a tree. Hummingbird was flabbergasted.

"How did you beat me? I am faster than you. I am smarter than you," Hummingbird exclaimed.

Heron was not surprised.
"You are? Really?
Then why did you rest
so much? I flew all day.
I flew all night. You wasted
your time sipping nectar."

Hummingbird did not
know what to say except,
"I guess you win."

15

From that day on, herons have owned all the rivers and lakes, eating all of the fish. And hummingbirds have fed only on nectar.